THE PRESENT

Michael Emberley

Little, Brown and Company

Boston Toronto London

Thank you, Andrea and Sarah

Also by Michael Emberley

Ruby

Dinosaurs! A Drawing Book

More Dinosaurs! and Other Prehistoric Beasts: A Drawing Book

First edition

Library of Congress Cataloging-in-Publication Data

Emberley. Michael.
   The present / Michael Emberley. — 1st ed.
      p. cm.
   Summary: After finally finding the perfect gift for his nephew's
birthday, a handy man wrestles with the temptation to keep the
present for himself.
   ISBN 0-316-23411-7
   [1. Gifts-Fiction.] I. Title.
PZ7.E566Pr   1991
[E] — dc20   90-6478

10 9 8 7 6 5 4 3 2 1

WOR

Published simultaneously in Canada
by Little, Brown & Company (Canada) Limited
and in Great Britain by Little, Brown and
Company (UK) Limited

Printed in the United States of America

Arne Hansen swung open the door of his fix-it shop, flooding the room with yellow light. He closed his eyes and let the spring sun warm his face. "Mmmmm," he sighed, taking a big bite of pickled herring sandwich.

Arne's quiet breakfast was interrupted suddenly by a strange noise —

Grind-rattle-squeak!   *Grind-rattle-squeak!*   *Grind-rattle-squeak!*

"Good morning, Lars," said Arne without opening his eyes.

"And a good morning to you," said Lars Pedersen, squealing to a halt. Arne winced. "I think your cycle wants a little oil."

"I'm a postman, not a handyman," said Lars, handing Arne a postcard. "It's from your sister. She has invited you to lunch on Saturday."

Arne tucked the last bit of sandwich into his mouth with a sticky thumb. "What else does it say?" he asked, not even looking at the card.

"How should I know?" said Lars quickly, turning a little pink in the ears. "I'm not the type that reads other people's mail."

"I believe you," said Arne politely.

Lars's ears turned red. "You'll need a present," he said.

Arne swallowed. "Present?"

"A birthday present for your nephew Tove," said Lars. "He'll be twelve on Saturday, did you forget?"

Now Arne was pink in the ears.

"It's market day in the village," said Lars, pedaling briskly off. "That's where *I* would look for a present."

"Of course, " mumbled Arne as Lars rattled away. "Brundby market. I'll find just the right birthday present for Tove at Brundby market." Now that it was on his mind, Arne could think of nothing else. So he left that moment for the village and began wandering slowly through the market stalls.

Arne felt certain that Brundby market was indeed the best place to look for a present for his nephew Tove. He spent hours carefully examining everything for sale. But nothing he saw seemed *just* the right present for a twelve-year-old-boy.

Then, at old Olaf Bork's stall, he picked something up.

"It's not new, but it's a good one," said old Bork in his gravelly voice.

Arne inspected the small, rust-covered pocketknife with his handyman's eye.

"Seventeen blades, tweezers, and a toothpick," grunted old Bork.

A wide grin slid slowly across Arne's face.

"Just right," he said.

Back at his shop Arne worked over all seventeen blades, even the tweezers and the toothpick, until they were clean, sharp, and polished. The knife looked brand new.

He tested each blade and was amazed by all the things the knife could do. He began thinking, "This would be a very handy tool to have in my shop." He held the knife. He fiddled with it. Arne's brain was working hard. "I wonder . . . ," he said to no one in particular, ". . . I wonder if this really is *just* the right present for a twelve-year-old b —"

At that moment, something in a cluttered corner of the shop caught Arne's eye. He squinted. He moved closer. He peered into the dark corner for a long time. Very slowly, a big grin slid across his face.

Taking only two breaks for pickled herring sandwiches, Arne set to work again, cleaning, bending, and adjusting late into the night. All his handyman knowledge, all his handyman skills, and every tool in his shop went into the task. It was dawn when he finally finished. He got halfway through a yawn before promptly falling asleep at his workbench.

"Good morning!" said Lars, pedaling up later that day. "Why it's, it's —"

"It's Tove's birthday present," said Arne, wiping the sleep from his eyes. He told Lars the story of the market, his long search, and his brilliant idea about the old bike. He decided not to mention the pocketknife.

"You are a wizard with a wrench," said Lars when Arne had finished. "It's a very nice present. But —"

"But?" said Arne.

"How are you going to get it to Silkborg? It's much too far to walk, and it certainly won't fit on the bus."

Arne looked blank.

"The easiest thing, of course," said Lars casually, "would be to ride it there."

"Ride it?" said Arne, as if he had been poked with a sharp stick.

"Ride it," said Lars. Both of them knew very well that Arne had never been fond of riding bicycles. "Look, riding a bike is easy. If I can do it, you can do it."

Arne's ears went pink, but he said nothing.

"Unless, of course, you can think of something else to give Tove, something you can carry with you."

Arne fiddled with the knife in his trouser pocket, but still said nothing.

"Well?" said Lars.

After a moment, a very long moment, Arne slowly, awkwardly, climbed on the bike. "Lars, I . . ."

"Just start pedaling," said Lars, giving Arne a push.

"That's it! That's it!" he shouted. "You're doing it!"

And he was . . .

. . . at first.

"Yes?" said Arne, not bothering to get up.

"I think you should consider giving Tove something else."

"Thank you, Lars," said Arne. "You've been very helpful."

"Anytime," said Lars cheerfully.

Arne practiced all afternoon. More than once he thought
of quitting. But by evening he was spending more time
on the bike than on the ground, and so he decided
he would give it a try.

On the morning of the party, Arne packed the pocketknife,
just in case he needed to make repairs, and a pickled herring sandwich.
Then, after a quick polish, he climbed on the bike and wobbled off.

The road to Silkborg passed right through Brundby village.
Arne's plan was to slip quietly down a side street. But before
he knew it, he had missed his turn, and found himself headed
straight into Market Square. Arne closed his eyes.

When Arne opened his eyes, he found himself headed out of town.
"That wasn't so bad," he thought.

Once on a quiet country lane, Arne began feeling the warm sun on
his back. The smell of fresh-cut grass filled his nose.

He spotted some storks winging home.

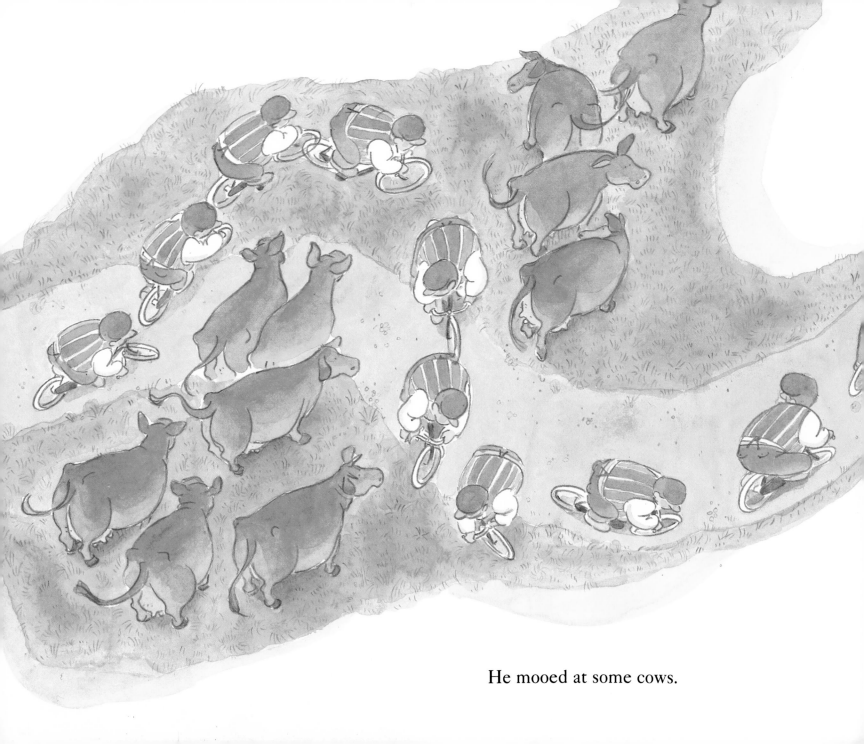

He mooed at some cows.

He climbed a small hill,

then zoomed down.
The wind sang in his ears.

He swung through some turns. He swooped and swerved. "Hmmm," said Arne, grinning, as he leaned into a particularly sharp bend. "I wonder if this really is *just* the right pres —"

Suddenly, a small boy ran out in the road.
Arne made an emergency stop.
"Uncle Arne, Uncle Arne!" shouted the boy.

Arne hadn't even noticed he was right in front of his sister's house.

"Uncle Arne," said his nephew Tove, jumping up and down. "Did you bring me something? Did you, Uncle Arne? A present?"

Arne got up. "Present?" he said. He looked at the bicycle.
He looked at Tove. "Present?" he said again.

There was what seemed to be a very long moment before Arne picked up the bike. He was trying to find the words, "Happy birthday, Tove," when he saw something he hadn't noticed up to now.

"Like my new bike?" chirped Tove excitedly. "I got it for my birthday. We'll go riding together after lunch. OK? You and me?"

Arne looked blank for a moment, his brain skipping gears. Then his hand found something in his pocket. The beginnings of a grin appeared at the corners of his mouth.

"For you," said Arne, slowly pulling out the carefully polished pocketknife. "Seventeen blades, tweezers, and a toothpick."

Tove stopped jumping. Arne flinched a little as the knife was taken from him by the small hand.

"Uncle Arne," Tove said. "It's . . . it's just what I wanted." He threw himself at Arne, surprising him. "Thank you, Uncle Arne," he whispered, "thank you, thank you, thank you."

Arne turned a little pink in the ears. "Happy birthday, Tove," he said, gently hugging back.

"Shall we go in?" said Arne, releasing his grip. "It's about time for some pickled herring sandwiches, I'd say."

"Come," said Tove tugging on Arne's sleeve.

"I have a better idea."

3